SHORT STORIES

from The Poor Man's Poet

1st run released November 2021 Hampton Roads, Virginia

copyright ©2021, Robert Kinard (Bobby K., the Poor Man's Poet) Williamsburg, Va
ISBN: 978-1-952773-45-7

Dedication

To Tabitha, my lovely wife – my five feet of paradise.

Contents

L.A.S.T. Revenge
I.

Monday morning, May 1ˢᵗ, 2022 outside the Clinton correctional facility; Leslie Allen Samuel-Tailer is being released for good behavior having served twenty-five years of a life sentence for murder. Leslie Allen Samuel-Tailer was the only prisoner being released today. Of course he will be out on parole. The only people waiting on him are his brother Darryl, Darryl's wife, Beverly, and just to the left of them is a writer by the name of Johnathan Oliver Berry. Leslie had told this writer that he'd be interested in his story – that he didn't want to miss it. J.O.B. is a retired FBI agent as of 15 years ago. Yet, for now, here Leslie stands 25 years later, alone, at the gate in front of an otherwise empty parking lot.

He had turned himself in after killing six of the eight men whom had been his bullies in their teenage years. He waited until after he'd served time in the military and traveled to other parts of the world like Germany, Turkey, and Italy. He then went and found them one by one. This was his long-awaited revenge; they had made his life miserable as a teenager, so he thought he'd return the favor as an adult.

Fifteen years ago, Leslie was not in the mood to talk about it, but over the years he has grown somewhat more cooperative, thoughtful and decided and contacted the same guy who was interested in the story as an FBI agent, now thinking it might make a good book someday. What the hell, it can't hurt to tell the story now. So, he and Johnathan decided that they would get together when he got out ... after the homecoming: a little get together with family.

Leslie and John will sit down and have a talk. Johnathan will come prepared with some tech to record, because he won't want to miss a thing. Leslie will begin to explain how it all started.

You see, we were living in a housing development called the Jefferson Projects our building was on the corner of South Division and Spring Street. There were twelve eight-story buildings on twenty-five acres of public property where no streets ran between the buildings. Some folks would call it the ghetto. It was on the lower east side of Buffalo.

I had more than my share of bullies. The thing was – I never went home and told my parents about them, I never once complained about having so many bullies. Sometimes my parents heard it from one of their neighbors. They heard about how I was being picked on and beaten up. My stepfather, a Navy vet and former boxer, asked if I was afraid to fight them?

I lied and said, "No,"

He said, "You know, if you take a big stick and knock one of them down, the rest will leave you alone." I think that might have been true in his day, but the truth was that my brother and I were outnumbered. There were times when my bullies would team up and work together, I walked into an ambush a few times.

We had a neighborhood gang called the Pythons they were the biggest street gang in the city of Buffalo.

"Okay, hey!" Jonathan interrupted, "how did you know that the Pythons where the biggest gang?"

Because they had meetings in their club house with members from the different parts of the city, and they used an empty apartment on the first floor of our building as the clubhouse. I was never picked on by the Pythons in fact there were a couple of times where they came to my defense. You see, I had a gang of bullies. I was out numbered, I had about eight of them altogether: two of them were twin brothers, Ronny and Johnny. Actually, on occasion their older brother Bill acted as a bodyguard for me and my brother. Bill kept his brothers from picking on us. Then there were

Moochie, Day'day, Carl, Lo'Lo, Re'Re and Godfrey. I couldn't even go to the neighborhood stores without being picked on and sometimes mugged and robbed by them.

Day'day, Re'Re and Lo'Lo used to hang out in front of the corner store called Ethel's Confectionery. So, most of the time I had to get past them to get in and out of the store. There was a beautiful black girl name Marcy, the daughter of the owner, and just like the saying goes she looked just like her mama. Marcy would be nice enough most of the time to get their attention; it would give me a chance to get away. When her mother was behind the counter I was on my own. I sometimes also went to another store called Danny's Deli.

Now, we lived in an eight-story building with a front and back stairwell and one elevator. I guess Moochie didn't have anything do the day he knocked on my apartment door and told me that I better come out side. I gave him a look that said 'Un-uhn' and closed the door. The second time he knocked on the door my mother answered, and the surprised Moochie pretended that he knocked on the wrong door. That same evening my stepfather came home from work and did his thing to relax which was to have my mother mix a few drinks for him and they would sit together in front of the stereo, talk and listen to some music. My mother liked to have dinner ready at 5:30pm so I came in early to wash my hands and get fed, only this time my stepfather called me over to talk and said, "I heard you've been having a rough time with some bullies... you don't look none the worse for wear. Would you like a little help?" and that's when he pulled out a pearl handed silver .38 caliber pistol and extended it to me handle first.

I hesitated for about two seconds and then reached for it, but he pulled it back asking me, "Do you think you know how to use it? And who would you shoot first? You must be ready to go to jail, if you're ready to shoot people. Maybe you'd better pick up a big stick or something."

3

Time went on, I was smart enough not to go to the same high school as my bullies. I grew up, graduated high school and joined the army. I was 20 years old when I signed up for six and served a four-year enlistment. While I was in the service, I learned to shoot weapons, and I took self-defense classes. All the while I was planning on how I could get back at all my former bullies. By now some years had passed, at least four of them, and I was sure that they would not have forgotten me, and what they did to me. I certainly would not ever forget them. I decided to make it my mission in life to get all of them one by one. It being four years, they wouldn't see me coming.

Now, I grew up in Buffalo, New York and it had not changed that much in the years that I was gone. I only had to look them up and I thought that maybe even one or two may still hang out somewhere together. I was looking forward to finding them. In this day and age, you would think people like Re'Re, Day'day and Lo'Lo would start going by their real first names. I will say this, that life has a way of getting back at you – or what goes around, comes around. It turns out Lo'Lo works for The Sanitation Department, we call it Buffalo Trash and Recycle. He's the guy you see jumping off the back of the truck to grab the trash cans and emptying them into the truck.

"Wait," said Johnathan, "tell me how you wound up *paying* for all of this?"

A CLASS OF BULLIES
(SURVIVING THE SIXTH GRADE)

As bullied boy Bobby
I was born and raised in the city of Buffalo, New York
I grew up on the lower east side.
My sixth-grade year of school, of what I can remember,
was the worst year of school.

In 1971 Public School Number Six was an elementary school. From kindergarten to the sixth grade Public School Number Six was on South Division and Pine Street, one block from my back door. I walked to and from school every day. The class was taught by Mr. Benson: a young white guy in need of a tan. In a classroom full of black children we had a few girls, but someone thought it would be better to move the three girls, and make it a class of all boys.

Now, un-like other classrooms that may have a bully or two, our class with Mr. Benson had six of them. I thought that was more bullies than the law allows... Actually, there were five; One kid did the 'go along to get along' thing just so he wouldn't get picked on like the rest of us.

Darryl had some size on him just a little bigger than the rest, and he was always wearing black leather gloves with half of the fingers cut off and the knuckles showing. The thing is that none of us wanted to be called a tattle tale or a snitch because it wasn't cool, and we didn't want to fight so, the bullying went on.

I lived in the projects, the Talbert Mall, where I already had
        a number of bullies.
Up until now, I didn't have any of them in my classroom.
Most of the boys in my class were the younger brothers of
        bullies and gang members.
Doing their best to follow in their footsteps.

5

One of the events not recorded in black history is that from the early-to-mid-60's to the mid 70's The Pythons were the largest street gang in the neighborhood and the city of Buffalo, New York. All with black jackets decorated with a large coiled Cobra on the back. It was a thing; all the gangs in the city of Buffalo, New York had their jackets. I thought it was funny how the companies that made the jackets sold them to every street gang in Buffalo, and yet managed to not get robbed by their customers.

In 1975 there was a black unity movement and all the street gangs got together and burned their jackets. But I guess that's another story for another time.

Well it was one thing to have a few bullies in your neighborhood,
     of which I had a few.
But to go to a school,
     where I wanted to be cool,
     and have to deal with bullies
     and gang member wannabees.
It was a daily challenge just make it to the 3 o'clock bell...

Most of the time right after lunch – when Mr. Benson turned his back to write something on the chalk board – that's when the punching, ear flicking and kicking started. He would turn his back for about thirty seconds. So, the bullies had to do their dirty work quickly and quietly. We didn't' have assigned seating so, in an effort to stop the bullies from messing with us, we'd move to a different desk each day – it was like we were playing musical chairs. Then the next time Mr. Benton turned his back a bully would move to a different desk.

It was like predator chasing prey.
One of my classmates raised his hand

and said he had to go to the bathroom.
The teacher would let us go one at a time.
Each was given the hall-pass
    a small block of wood
    with the word hallpass carved on it.
We carried that when we went to the restroom.

Only he didn't come back,
    this boy went down the hall,
    and walked into another classroom
    pleaded his case.
And the teacher let him stay.

I don't know if Mr. Benson didn't know how to deal with this
    or if the man was just slow.

It was a kid named Kevin, who also lived in the projects, who was sitting behind me, he poked me with a ruler and said in a low voice, "Where's my money? You better have my money tomorrow." He was there the day when his older brother caught me on my way home from the store, and took fifty cents from me. So, now it's monkey-see monkey-do – or at least he was trying to.

When we went to gym class, that's when the bullies had a free hand to do their thing. While we were playing basketball Kevin tried to play the tough guy. He felt on my pockets, but you can't take what I don't have, telling me that I'd better have his money tomorrow.

After seeing a few guys get punched and slapped and no fighting back the white Gym teacher saw what was going on and asked me, "What's with the guys rough housing?" I shrugged my shoulders because I couldn't tell him that we were being bullied.

Because it wasn't cool to be called a snitch.

I came home a few times with a swollen lip,
    I lied and told my mother that I slipped
    and fell.
I was looking none the worse for wear.
    I wasn't bleeding
    so my mother didn't say anything.

    As luck would have it, I was walking home from school, and there was a quarter laying on the ground like someone choose that day to lose one. I went on to school the next day and waited until Kevin said, "Where's my money?"

    I gave him the quarter and we were cool after that; he didn't try to get more money from me. I think he was surprised that I gave it to him.

    Mr. Benson caught on to this, or he had had enough. When he turned around one day and saw two of his students with tears running down their faces. He had no problem figuring out that it was the two angels, complete with halos, setting behind them. One kid began to whimper as his bottom lip began to swell. The angel sitting behind him started to grin; He had just taken that kid's money.

    So, Mr. Benson's solution was to put all six angels in a separate row on the right side of the classroom, with a row of empty desks between us and them. For about two weeks, the bullies were bored, having only their classwork to do and no one to pick on. We were starting to have some fun in class. The bullies actually had to wait – for gym class or to find us after school before they could do their thing.

Fear being my main motivator,
    my one block walk
    became a three-block run.
Needless to say,

I had to go out my way,
      just to avoid bullies and a beat down.
This was also the start of my short career
as a neighborhood track star.

    What you have to understand is that the bullies came in a
group, or a gang. Whenever you got up the nerve to fight one you'd
never find them alone, so you couldn't stand up to just one. This
was about a year before the start of America's martial art movie craze.
There were a few mornings where they caught me on my way to
school, and of course, there was that morning my mother caught me
taking a different route to school.
    The day came that some students fear, and some teachers
look forward to. At the end of the second quarter: Open House...
The day when everyone's mother came to school and had a chat with
teachers. The parents learned how well – or how poorly – their
children were doing in school because report cards didn't tell the
whole story. Yet, for Mr. Benson, this is a day that will live... In
infamy.
    All six mothers, Mrs. Ethel Chelcy, my Mother and the
assistant principal had surrounded him in front of his classroom
door. They wanted to know why he was picking on their six well
behaved boys. Needless to say, he couldn't get a word in edgewise.

The mothers who came to rise hell,
Called him everything but a child of God.
Hearing the colorful name calling in the hallway.
      the angels were smiling,
      and giving each other high fives.

    By the end of the chaotic huddle, which lasted all of fifteen
minutes, Mr. Benson was ordered to put the boys back with the rest
of the class. The assistant principal told the women that she's going

to have a long talk with Mr. Benson, and then called out all six
angels, sending them home with their mothers.

For the next two weeks we had a parade
  of substitute teachers.
  who had all learned the names of all six angels.
The bullies didn't miss a chance to harass us and heckle
  the substitute teachers.
When Mr. Benson returned,
  wearing a very nice tan.
He'd got his hair cut and was sporting sunglasses.
  the kind that flips up.
We didn't recognize him
  standing in the back
We were behaving the way
  we did when had a sub
  teaching for the day,
Then Levi recognized him –
  Mr. Benson standing in the back of the class.
We all had an oh shit moment.
Everybody got back in their seat.
And it got real quiet, real fast.

Although for me it was the worst year of school, I know for a
fact that all of the boys in that class passed to the seventh grade. By
the time I was a senior year of high school three of those bullies were
in juvenile detention and two of them had died in gang fights.

12-12-12

Midnight, on the 12th of December 2012 was the end of the world
                                                as the Mayans had seen things.
There are many who believe that history and the Mayans
                                                                got it wrong.
I am not one of them, but I am here narrating this list of events.

Murphy's Law states: What can go wrong, will go wrong,
                                        at the worst possible moment.
Well, it's not that they were wrong.
Let's just say, someone
                        who claimed to be an expert on Mayan language.
Misinterpreted the Mayans symbols,
                                and no one caught the mistake.
The 12th of December 2012 on the Mayans' calendar
                was not the end of the world, but the end of something else?
Twelve o'clock midnight on the east coast of North America.
On December 12, 2012
                                        it started snowing, kind of hard.
Cars, buses and trucks almost all modes of transportation
                        in and around the cities and around the world
                                                for that matter
                                suddenly cutoff, slowed and stopped.

Electric vehicles, those that weren't stuck in traffic,
                        managed to get around and go about their way.
The clicking you heard was people trying to start their cars.
                                aircraft, and all powered flight,
                                both commercial and military
                to the nightmare of all pilots and air traffic controllers
        found themselves flying and directing new metal gliders.

11

Many people were not very fortunate
                 as aircraft everywhere started falling out of the sky.
The death toll is in the hundreds as they crash-land.
Some of the lucky ones already in traffic patterns,
                       in and around the airports
                manage to land on un-used run ways,
      and some even managed to land on the nearby Highways.
Any expressways and freeways became needed runways.
           to the relief and applause of all the passengers on aboard.
Any of the people aboard who had some doubts about a
            supreme being, found a reason to believe in the one.
Those aircraft already on the ground couldn't take off as
               the engines stopped running
         stranding a great many numbers of people
       too many to count at airports all over the world.

Cars stalled in parking lots and gas stations.
Calls for help went out everywhere...
The Police, Fire Department and all first responders
              were all just as stuck as everyone else.
The News and Print media started shooting live video
            from their building windows.
In the city that never sleeps,
       in an effort to keep order
          the New York City Chief of Police,
      Marquis Garner
put officers on horseback and foot patrols.
Although the subway was unaffected,
           both freight and passenger trains
      that were in motion, once they lost their momentum,
          slowed and came to a stop...
       puzzling both Engineers and Conductors.

Things got stranger as the sun rose.
The same things were happening in the Mid-West
              and on the West coast. And eventually all over the planet.

Explosives everywhere, dynamite, TNT and C-4,
    to the surprise of many explosive and demolition experts wouldn't
                                                              work.
Those people with a cause or a mission,
                        what some people would call terrorists,
                  were finding that their tools aren't working.
The victims that had been taken
                  and strapped or fitted with vests loaded with C-4
                  or other homemade explosives got to laugh a little
                        as they pulled them off and walked away.

People in a dilemma trying to commit suicide by cop.
                  and those trying to take out a lot of people with them. ..
They were also surprised when,
            in public places, people carrying what they supposed to be an
                        exploding backpack, pressed the button
                              and nothing happened.

One call for the police when a husband took his wife hostage:
                  A former Marine in what is a dangerous situation
                                    for all concerned.
He held his wife by the neck in a full-nelson chokehold.
                        with a live grenade ready to pull the pin –
If the police don't give him some room to think
                        he's going to bring this all to an end.
A police negotiator is trying to talk him down,
                              but he's not having it.
                        with that thousand-yard stare that
                              you only see in the movies.

13

He pulled the pin and drop the grenade at their feet.
Grenade hits the floor and rolls for about a foot and a half.
And... and nothing happens...
A few seconds pass and still nothing...
They look at the grenade like an egg that didn't break.

and then for some reason
the husband starts to laugh
turning his wife loose.
The policemen smile and before they can

take the man into custody.
The wife who's had enough, goes off on

her mixed-up better half.
She's had some self-defense training.
Before they were dating, she was a brown belt in karate.
The police have to rescue the husband

from his now very pissed off wife.
She, starting to beat the snot out of her husband,

and stress relief got a few people laughing.

Elsewhere in the world shoot outs suddenly stop.
You could hear triggers being pulled and nothing happening.
It took a few moments before all sides

catch on that their weapons won't work.
Someone pulls out a knife,

and this gives birth to new track stars.
Now that police have to chase people on foot and
rely on their nightsticks and tasers to keep order.

Western North Pacific Ocean,

somewhere east of the Philippines
One half mile below the surface at the Mariana trench,

Rift Industries latest state of the art boomer,
the **U.S.S. Shade Palmer**

– next generation ballistic missile submarine,
under the command of Captain Chrissney Coleman.
somewhere in her years of service as a warrior
she picked up the nick name BB
(as in Battle Bitch.)
Rumor has it that no one has ever called her that
to her face   without receiving grievous bodily harm.
A few moments after everything went dead quiet.
"Captain we have lost propulsion."
Captain Coleman caught off guard.
"What do you mean we lost propulsion?"
"Our main engines have stop running
and we can't get them to start.
Engineering is working on it.
They say the electric motors .
are un-affected."
"Ok, then switch to the electric motors.
And take us to periscope depth,
I need to bounce a message off satellites,
and tell somebody about their new toy."

The White House, 9:00 AM, members of the president's staff
manage to meet in the oval office to try and find some answers.
"Madam President
the best our scientists have figured out
is that there is no combustion happening anywhere
on the entire planet.
Electricity still works,
along with lights,
electric cars and some trains.
Not one to sit and think
Donna M. Carter likes to pace back and forth
in front of her desk.

Her second year in office, and she was hoping
no major world events would take place on her watch.
"How is this possible?
Do we have any idea as to what's causing this?"
"No. Ma'am!
Our scientists say
they aren't sure what's causing it.
They're working trying to find some answers.
Madam President, most of America won't be going to work
this morning,
and a great number of people working third shift
are stuck at work and can't go home.
People are stranded in their cars everywhere,
on the road, in airports, in planes and at train stations.
The only exception being electric vehicles;
they somehow still work.
Luckily, there are a few in the motor pool.,
so we were able to gather the Joint Chiefs.
Our E.O.D. experts are saying that C-4,
Nitroglycerin, dynamite, and TNT
have somehow become inert.
And that Gunpowder may as well be Talcum powder.
nothing will explode or go boom.
Electricity and gravity haven't been affected.
The phones are still working
This means our military is unarmed?
Since weapons won't work, ma'am, there is no war,
and a worldwide cease fire has been unofficially declared
whether anybody wants one or not.
At least for the short term, any fighting will have to be
hand to hand.
Transportation as a whole
has come to an almost complete stop.

16

The military has some electric vehicles;
we have ships floating out there having
to depend on what few electrical engines that they have,
basically, they are running on batteries
Our Fifth, Sixth and Seventh Fleets are managing
to hold their own, and are awaiting orders.
The Coast Guard has ships with electric engines
they even had to save a few of their own ships."
"Gentlemen it seems
  that in some ways we have been pushed
  back to the nineteenth century.
I want to see how wide spread this is.
Let's get the other world leaders on the phone.
  I want to know if they have come up with anything,
  and while you're at it get me the pope
  on my privet line.
I think we could use some special help on this one."

The Vice-President Tabitha Kinard walks in,
  a (BBW) Beautiful Black Woman, all business.
"Excuse Me Ma'am," after having her own meeting
      with a few agencies with acronyms.
"Gentlemen I have it on good authority
  that all our larger toys in the weapons stock pile
    do not work.
It's only a theory,
  but we have reason to believe that even
  the neutron bomb just became
  a very expensive paperweight."
"What this means, gentlemen,
  said the President,
    "is that the playing field is level right now,
      I don't want to play catch up,

17

and since we don't have any idea
how long this will last,
I have to deal with the upcoming food shortage problem."

12 Days, 12 hours, 12 minutes, Christmas day:
The weather being what it is,
Mother Nature is free to do as she pleases.
She made her feelings felt in the form of snow,
falling a few inches in some places,
and several feet in others.
In the cities of Buffalo, New York; Chicago, Illinois;
Detroit, Michigan and Washington, DC
The snow fell in record amounts.
Left unattended snow piled up, and with no school,
the kids and some adults had a ball.
The news and information media were doing what they could
to report what they could, like record snowball fights.
People had been out of work for almost two weeks now,
and with no snow removal some electric vehicles
are getting stuck in the snow.
People want to know how long with this last?

Christmas day at the White house.
It being a holiday, Raymond Carter, the first gentlemen,
let Donna sleep late.
All of fifteen minutes
after waiting for Donna to make her appearance.
Sixteen-year-old Wendel, the President's first-born son
opened his Christmas present
of his very own hunting rifle.
Something he had asked for
since before
the family moved in,

18

but right now, Donna wasn't worried
because guns, for some reason,
won't fire.

Or so she thought
as her son, Wendel, sitting under the Christmas tree
opened his present,

and since weapons won't fire
Donna bent the rules a little bit
about weapons at the White house.
To the shock and surprise that had Donna, and all secret service is
when Wendel took aim at the star on the top of the Xmas tree,
the weapon fired.

L.A.S.T. Revenge
II.

Well, once when I was on leave in the Army, I went to a casino out West. I won enough money to do what I did. I saved some of the money and I do mean I put away a lot of cash. I even took on a part time job after duty hours as a bartender at a nightclub. I took my time to buy weapons and other equipment that would help me get the job done. Then, all I did was go on line; there are plenty of web sites that will tell you what you want to know about anybody. Really even the phone company's white pages. The city's web page helped me learn which days and which garbage route Lo'Lo would be on so I could pick the time and the place. I had a rifle with a silencer so I won't draw attention when I fired the shot. Lo'Lo's first name was Logan, he was called Lo'Lo as a baby name and it stuck with him.

The route the trash truck was on took them near a construction work site and the truck would stop there to pick up just one trash can and that's when Lo'Lo would take a leak in one of the portable bathrooms. So, this time I managed to be on the roof top of a building about fifty yards away. As Lo'Lo went into the portable bathroom – just as he was pulling the door closed – I put a bullet in the back of his head.

No one heard the shot, and because of the noise of the truck engine no one heard Logan fall dead in the bathroom. Logan had been dead in the bathroom for forty-five minutes before someone got tired of waiting for the bathroom and got the nerve to go in and find him there, dead.

Johnathan asked, "Did you stay there the whole time?"

"Yes, I stayed until cops got there. Remember Logan was on his trash run. After I got him I moved on to who was next on my list and, as it turned out, Moochie's first name was Montel. His full name was Montel Ulysses David. Right, His Initials are M. U. D. I think that's why he stuck with Moochie.

Moochie worked for the cleaning department at Bethlehem Steel not far from Buffalo, in the city of Lackawanna. Bethlehem Steel employs about 180,000 people, among whom two of my other former bullies also worked. Still, I planed to get them one at a time; If I have to, then two at a time. So after doing a little investigating, which did take some time – about three weeks, I out found that Moochie works the night shifts from 11:00 PM to 7:00 AM. His drive home was like any other morning's drive, except this time there was a van in his parking spot. It was marked Pest Extermination "Get rid of your old pests once and for all – Satisfaction Guaranteed!" The van was backing out, so he waited and let the van out. Then he parked his car and went inside the house. When he closed the door, he noticed a funny smell. Not sure where it was coming from, he went to check out that odor. He barely noticed he was getting a little light headed with the smell of this gas. Thinking he'd better open a window. He tried to open one in the living room, and found it stuck then he tried to open a window in the kitchen. Now by this time he was getting pretty dizzy.

What he didn't know was that the gas was cyanide. I had put a small cylinder in his vent. He started to cough, then decided he should get out of the house. However, when he got to the door it wouldn't open. His vision went dark and he fell dead to the floor.

Driving the van down the road with a smile on my face, happy with myself for rigging the windows and the front and back doors of the house to not open. You see Cyanide gas is used to get rid of pests and that's what I use it for.

Johnathan asked, "How did you rig the front door?"
"Oh, that was easy, but I'll leave it for you to figure that out."

<u>Kidnapping Mistake</u>

In a bold attempt to extort money from James P. Bartlett III, a corporate executive – C-E-O of a marketing and advertisement firm – Ronny and Moe, a couple of bad guys, kidnapped some senior citizens; namely his Grandparents from the Better Days retirement and rest home which recently came under new management.

Why the grandparents? Because his parents lived in a gated community and thus, the grandparents would be easier to take, or so Ronny and Moe thought.

Both Margaret and James Bartlett Sr. were 85 years old. They went willingly because Ronny and Moe were dressed like the rest of the rest home employees. Ronny and Moe didn't see that certain look the senior citizens exchanged with each other nor the smirks on their faces.

When the elderly two almost fell on each other and them coming out of the elevator the bad boy wannabes didn't notice that their pockets had been picked; Not that Ronny and Moe had any real money. Mrs. Bartlett was nice enough to let them keep the spare change that she found. Ronny and Moe gathered their bags unaware that they had been picked almost clean.

The van ride to the ship was nice, and Mrs. Bartlett spent the day talking about her grandson almost all of the way the pier. Mr. and Mrs. Bartlett were given tickets and loaded aboard a large ocean liner for a two-week senior cruise to the Islands.

The couple were told to have a good time because this was a surprise from their grandson James. Ronny, thinking that Margaret and James Bartlett Sr. were slow when it comes to technology, took their phones and gave them simple-to-use flip phones that could only call Ronny and Moe in case they had any questions.

For Ronny and Moe everything was going as planned. As the Mr. and Mrs. were senior citizens, Ronny had listed himself as part of the family that should be kept informed of his family member's activities. Ronny used the old man's cell phone to call James P. Bartlett III to make his list of demands. Ronny had thought that James would be surprised to hear from whom he thought would be his grandparents, however it was the receptionist who answered the phone with, "Bartlett advertising how may I direct your call?"

Caught off guard and not expecting this Ronny said, "Let me speak to James Bartlett III,"

"Whom shall I say is calling?"

"Look! It's very important that I speak with him right damn now! I'm someone who has a very important possession of his." The line was disconnected. Ronny called back saying, "Hey Lady, this isn't a prank call! Let me speak to James P. Bartlett III right now!"

"Hold please."

Then, after a few seconds of elevator music, "Hello! Who the hell is this, and what do you mean you have something of mine?"

"My name is not important. If you don't do what I say, you'll never see your grandparents again!"

"How do I know you have my grandparents? Tell me something about them."

"Well, your grandfather is an ornery old fart with a beard and a head full of white hair. He looks pretty good for his age. He tried to hire me to be your assistant, said you needed one, badly, and that you won't get anything done until you pull your head out of your ass, and take your foot out of your mouth – in that order. Your grandmother, even with her white hair in a bun, looks like she has won a couple of beauty pageants in her time, and for an old lady she is still built like a brick shit-house with brand new doors. Your grandmother, who likes to talk, went on to tell me how you got the football team to beat up a few bullies in high school. She even told us how you, arm wrestled a cheerleader's dad for a chance to go out with her."

James P. Bartlett III started to laugh, "Well now, let tell you what you're in for. They are two of a kind, the definition of eccentric, and somewhat senile. Any and all domestic help refuse to work for them. They have been put out of four rest homes, and word had gotten around about them. I had to buy a rest home so that they can't be kicked out. They are always up to something, they like to have fun at your expense, and since you don't know what you're in for, let me enlighten you..."

"First, I'll bet you don't have your wallet,
And if you do, there's nothing in it."
Ronny pulled his wallet out to find it empty.
"I'm going to wish you the best of luck
with those two,"
And with that he hung up.
After hanging up the phone he told his secretary
to give Linda,
his favorite private investigator,
a call, "and see
what my grandparents are up to."

It didn't take long, because the next day Ronny and Moe's phones were ringing off the hook. The ship had run into some bad weather. The first call came from James Senior; he was seasick and he wanted to get off this boat. Well according to the cruise director, it turned out he got mad when he couldn't buy the ship, and the Captain asked James senior to leave the bridge.

Then the wife called complaining about a voluptuous woman throwing herself at her husband. "If she bumps into my husband one more time I'm going to do my best to lighten the ship's load by throwing the big bitch overboard."

James Bartlett III was on the phone with Linda the P.I., who had to hear about how his grandparents made a mess of themselves jumping in a van and driving off with two men dressed like employees.

Ronny got another call from the ship's cruise director about the couple fighting with other couples. Ronny learned many reasons why senior citizens are not kidnapped. The cruise director called again complaining about James senior after he had insisted on trying to buy one of the islands. "And he keeps asking where's Gilligan?" At which point the Cruise director was ready to put him off the ship. Ronny, feeling that he had bitten off more than he could chew, began wondering what he could do.

Ronny and Moe were staying in an apartment on the lower East-side of the town. Ronny heard a knock at their door and didn't want to answer it, fearing that life wasn't bad enough. He heard in a loud voice a man saying, "Open up, it's the F.B.I."

<u>In the Year 2525</u>

In this clean-climate future
time travel is, what some like to say,
a common comical conveyance.
Too many people find themselves
in embarrassing situations.
Time Travel is a commodity sold like airfare.
Now that people have flying cars
with the new, safe smart technologies,
clean air is a standard in the aviation industry.
Cadillac, Lexus, and Ferrari, among others,
have joined the aviation industry.
Now that we have air filtering electric engines
complete with artificial intelligence
our cars do more than talk, they take us
comfortably where we want to go.
Now that we are no longer traveling on the ground,
car accidents have long been a thing of the past.
We can't forget that we've also found that
we are not alone in the universe.
Just like New Years and Mardi Gras,
there is an annual visit from a friendly alien race
called the Elpoep; they evolved from Plant life.
Purple-colored humanoids with double pupiled, turquoise eyes,
they are from the planet Fluoressa; it is only a light year away.
After we got over the big deal of us not being alone in the universe,
we first had to get out of our own way,
and convince the right people and countries
that would not let them in or over their air-space –
that the Elpoep, did not come to take over.
The purple people came in peace.
The Elpoep, came to Earth as environmental emissaries.

Showing us how to clean up, what there was to clean up
of the planet Earth.
I do mean that with their help in a short period of time
of about two years, with a planet wide million-dollar cleanup
the air and water all over the planet,
is back to the state that can only described as preindustrial.
If you can imagine getting a breath of fresh air
everywhere you go, all over the planet.
All creek, river and lake water is clean and safe to drink
no matter where you go.
They did not just envision clean oceans.
Plastic pollution has become a thing of the past.
There's practically no pollution all over the planet.
Wild life all over the planet is starting to grow in numbers.
Even those that were near extinction are making a comeback,
and with that the Elpoep have chosen to make earth
a vacation destination, becoming our first intergalactic tourists.
Now we still have a few flying UFO's, but the Purple people
Tell us that the UFO's will reveal themselves when they are ready.
The Elpoep, or the purple people,
are drawn to all the major waterfalls.
They are also fascinated with the fact that, unlike on their planet,
our trees do not walk,
and we have people living in treehouses.
Plans for paying a visit to the Elpoep home world
Is in the works as we speak,
and with technical help from the Elpoep,
NASA has made some improvements in space travel.
Meanwhile, we have even invited the purple people
to participate in the Olympics,
and with that some new events
have been added to the Olympics,
welcoming the purple people to our planet.

The Elpoep like to take part
in the fresh-air competition.
We honor them by taking part
in single paddle boat racing and unicycling,
and so far, they remain unbeaten.

Now for some people, and the Elpoep
time travel is considered
to be a matter of entertainment.
It's like going to a theme park,
only we don't close after dark.
There are a few companies
that provide these forms of entertainment.
This is but one of many infomercials.

Here at EON
there's no time like
the past, present *or* future.
Let us take you,
where you want to go!
... on or off planet.

EON...
A Personal Time Travel Company.
Take time, to travel in time.
Here at Eon
We can take you
where you want to go –
when you want to go.
We'll have you there
when you want to be there.:
enjoying your involvement
in future activities.

Note: by law, trips to the past
are observation only.
You cannot interfere:
meaning you cannot change
the past, *Period*.
If something happened
like an inconvenience –
you lost money,
or you lost the fight –
you cannot change the past,
your life, or that of a family member.
As much as it pains us,
you cannot travel to the future
to get a cure for some
infectious disease,
that a family member
died from in the past.
We're sorry... but here at EON,
you *can* see how your parents
Or grandparents met.
With the option of
time-lapse time travel,
you can even watch
your parents grow up.
Since you have the time,
you can travel back
through your entire family line.
In our time travel facilities
we can take you anywhere
you need to go, and have you there
when you need to be there,
... on or off planet.

The Poor Man's Poet

When you've had enough,
and seen enough
we can bring you back
at the push of a button.
Our time travel facilities
are just as comfortable
as sitting at home in your living room.
For anyone traveling to the past,
we even have a remote control.
Here at Eon, we can give you the option
of sending you in holographic form.
That's right you can be
projected like a hologram
and watch everything
as it takes place;
no one will see you.
All part of the EON
personal time travel experience.
Since we now live on
The Moon, Mars and a few Asteroids,
The sky is no longer the limit.
We can even let you have a replay
of an athletic or historic event.
Now, for those of you
with the idea of traveling
to the future just so you can get
the local lottery numbers,
we are sorry;
we can't let you do that,
for that, too, is an attempt to change the past,
and that is against the law
of time travel.

There is a time travel enforcement bureau,
and they really keep track of time.
It's called Decades and, of course,
it's run by our planetary government
because Uncle Sam always has the time
to keep time in line.
A Decades time enforcement team
will show up and correct
any time discrepancies.
Here at Eon,
we won't lose track of time.
You can travel to near-infinity.
We have an automatic timer
set to bring you back.
That is for those of you
who have a habit,
of getting lost in time.
EON...
A Personal Time Travel Company.

L.A.S.T. Revenge
III.

Then there was the maintenance man working the midnight shift on the Peace Bridge. There was no moon that night, and there was a foggy mist hanging over the bridge. The lights on the bridge are bright enough to see where you're going, but not much else. Damon, otherwise known as Day'Day is still new to the job although he's been there for a couple of months. That night he was assigned to check on a few things along the length of the bridge. Alone, he walked down the length of the bridge. From the American side, in the fog, I looked like a stranger walking from the other end.

I called out his name, "Hey, Day'Day is that you?"

"Yeah! Who are you, and why are you on the bridge this time of night?"

"The question is, do you remember someone you bullied back in the day named Leslie?"

Damon stopped right in his tracks. He saw a man headed towards him dressed in black and the flash of a hunting knife in his hand. We were just about in the middle, but still on the American side, and Damon turned to run through the fog. I guess he heard I was coming. I was just a little faster. Just as I was about to grab him I said, "Payback's a bitch, Mutha–" but before I could finish calling him a name, he put one hand on the railing and hopped off the bridge.

Yelling as he went down Damon, formally known as Day'Day, let the world know he didn't know how to swim. He went with the current and didn't get far down. He went down drowning in the foggy night.

Johnathan asked, "How quickly did you go from one the next?"

33

"Sometimes weeks passed as I went from one to the next. For the most part they are not in touch with each other."

Finding a need for knowledge Re'Re, whose first name was Renae, had been going to training school. He was trying to become a repairman: a regular Mr. fix-it for General Electric, learning to fix and repair washers, and dryers, and other appliances. He didn't know how I planned to fix him.

Renae drove a 1990 Blue Buick LeSabre. On his way home it's just his luck that, with my help, he had a flat tire. While he was in class, I helped myself to the air valve on one of his tires with a pair of needle nose pliers. I pulled just enough to give them a decent slow leak. He pulled over on the side of the road of the Interstate. I had been following far enough back to make it look like I just happened to be coming down the road and see him broken down. I pulled over, and we did the catching up routine that people do when they haven't seen each other in quite a while. He didn't know that I had been following him for some time, weeks even, and had learned his routine.

While he was changing his flat tire. I reminded him that he used to be one of my bullies as a teenager, I never saw a smile fall off someone's face so fast. We were on the right-hand side of the car, where people couldn't see us clearly from the road.

He was down on one knee changing the tire. He said, "Hey man you know that we didn't know any better."

That's when I put a bullet in his right ear. A .45 caliber with a silencer so's not to draw any attention to us. I sat him with his back to the car. It looked like he had fallen asleep. I took what little cash he had and his ID. He used to take my money when my parents sent me to the store, so now we're even. I left him there on the interstate where the state police found him.

An Alcoholic's Game

Good afternoon everyone and welcome to those of you just tuning in to the first mighty major league hall of fame baseball game, here at Firewater Stadium in Williamsburg, Virginia, where fans of alcohol and alcoholic fans have been waiting to wet their whistle!

In this fermenting feud, it is a battle of the beverages
Booze versus Beer.
No matter which side you're rooting for,
you have only yourself to blame
for any hangovers after the game.
I am your host Dry Martini
and with me in the booth
is my main man Vermouth.

Right now, walking up to the pitcher's mound
      with their unique sound.
We have the C-P-K trio,
Coke, Pepsi & Kool-Aid
Singing a cappella the teetotalers tune,
The national anthem of refreshments

We are refreshments,
Word has gotten around,
We are refreshments,
The best thing in town!
Think of us first
To quench your thirst!
We are refreshments,
Word has gotten around
We are refreshments
The best thing in town!

You love it a lot
when we hit the spot
Let me hear everybody say
Aaaahhhh!!!

The honor of throwing out the first pitch today is Laurent Perrier,
Not a bad arm, for someone
with water and Champaign
                            to his name.
Now, as the game gets underway,
taking the outfield in Green and white
                                        pinstripe   uniforms
Is the Beer team. Millers, Mickey's, Samuel Adams and Guinness
with Coors on shortstop.
Fosters on first, Becks on second, and Pabst Blue Ribbon on third.
On the mound, ready to pitch
is the brew master,
Budweiser, The King of Beers.
He's only been around since 1876
and catching for the Beer team is Amstel.
Starting lineup for the Hard Liquor team
wearing white uniforms with red pinstripes
        is Tango Ray (Tanqueray),
        Courvoisier
and Remy Martin.
With Hard hitting Hennessy batting cleanup.
The umpires officiating the game today
is four members from the 21st amendment.
Start of the first inning.
Stepping up to the plate batting first is Mr. Gin himself
Tango Ray.
A seasoned player he's been around since 1831
one of many spirits from Scotland.

Budweiser goes through the motions,
he winds up, and here is the pitch...
Looks like he let loose with a flash of lite lager.
A fastball just barely inside for strike one.
Tango Ray didn't even see it.
But it made him flinch,
the frown on Tango's face says he's not happy.
Budweiser smiles gets the signal he wants
winds up for the pitch,
and throws a lightning Lite Ale outside for the ball one.
Stepping back from home plate,
Tango takes a few swings
confident that the next pitch won't get past him.
Stepping up to the plate tango is ready.
Budweiser throws a wild fermented screwball,
the umpire yells, "strike two!!"
"Hey, Tango!" Tango turns and sees his coach
standing in the dugout.
Captain Morgan touches the brim of his cap and smiles at Tango,
and Tango Ray touches the brim of his cap and smiles back.
Budweiser winds up and throws a Pale Ale curveball.
Tango bunts, the ball bounces halfway
between home plate and first base,
with Tango sprinting like a track star,
Amstel moves after the ball
              and throws to Fosters on first.
Tango Ray dives and touches the bag
just before the ball gets there. He's safe on first.
Standing up dusting himself off.

Courvoisier, one of the Cognac brothers,
steps up to the plate ready for anything.
Budweiser winds up and throws a Stout changeup.

That's low and outside for ball one.
Budweiser is ready, goes through the motions
and throws a Brown Ale slider,
Courvoisier swings – a loud crack of the bat.
The ball, going deep-right, hits the wall,
Courvoisier hits a double, as the skies begin to darken.
Courvoisier makes it to second base
                        as thick gray clouds start rolling in.
That put Tango Ray on third.
Remy Martin comes up to bat,
          another of the Cognac   brothers.
He's been around since 1724
          He takes a few swings
and he is ready to turn anything
over the plate into a home run.

Budweiser winds up for the pitch
          and throws a Belgian style curveball
          for strike one.
Budweiser is in the zone.
  winds up and throws a Pale Ale curveball.
Remy swings and connects, the ball bounces Just short of the pitcher
and over his head,
falling near second base.
Beck's catches the ball and throws it home,
Tango Ray who doubles back to third.
          Amstel throws to Fosters on first.
Remy makes it there in time.

With the bases loaded, hard-hitting Hennessey comes up to bat.
Hennessey, a no-nonsense player,
been around since 1765.
Yet, do not let this Frenchman fool you.

Hennessey takes a few practice swings,
then he points at center field with his bat,
Hennessey is a homerun hitter.
He then takes his stance ready, as a lite rain begins to sprinkle.
    Standing on the mound Budweiser looks for his signal,
winds up and throws
    what looks like an
Olde English Torpedo for strike one.
Hennessey watched it go by with an unimpressed look on his face.
Budweiser winds up and throws a lightning Lager,
Hennessey swings, cracking his bat, knocking the ball out of the park
and into orbit.
Hard-hitting Hennessey did it again.

Clearing the bases with the score now 4 & O
as the rain comes down like someone turned on the shower.
The game is on hold as people run for cover.
After about a half hour of hard rain,
                Mother Nature clearing the air
and most of the seats,
slowly lets the sun part the clouds
    and the rain stopped.
The ground crew pulls the tarps off the field
    and the officials are ready to pick up the game
    right where it left off.

It's still top of the first, with a score 4 & O.
The players take to the field to get this ballgame under way.
Budweiser did a few warm-up pitches and is ready to go.
There are still more than a few hardcore fans
       in the stadium: sitting in stands
with their umbrellas and rain gear.
Just enough to let you see how full the place is.

First one up to bat after the rain delay score (4-0)
is Mr. Rum himself Don Bacardi
He has been around since 1862.
Budweiser goes through the motions and here's the pitch...
It's a Stout changeup,
Bacardi swings and it's a pop fly to deep centerfield.
Samuel Adams is right there
as it falls right into his glove for an out.
This brings Moonshine get right up to bat.
Some people call him Hooch, and a few other colorful names.
If you're not careful, Mr. Get-right can be a headache
        waiting to happen.
Hooch is the wildcard of the team having been legalized
in most countries around the world.
Moonshine walks up to the home plate
with the bat resting on his shoulder
 like he does not have a care in the world.
He takes his stance waiting for the ball.
Budweiser winds up and throws a Brown Ale Slider.
Hooch swings and hits a ground ball to left,
between second and third base.
And is picked up by Coors at shortstop
        who makes the throw to first,
            just barely beating Moonshine for the second out.

Elijah Craig steps up to bat.
Budweiser on the mound looking for his signal,
        gets the signal he wants,
winds up and throws an Olde English Torpedo for strike one.
Budweiser going through the motions and throws a brown ale slider
(Mr. Bourbon) Elijah Craig is ready he swings and it's a pop fly!
With a flash of lightning and crack of thunder

both Mother Nature and Elijah Craig
make their intentions known.
The ball is sailing deep into left field
      where Miller manages to catch it for out number three.
This time Mother Nature gives us a light show,
      with a few bolts of lightning
      and loud rumbles of thunder
      and once again the rain has everyone
                          run   for cover
and the game is called.

Mother Nature closes the curtains again.
The sky darkens, and everyone can see and hear the flash of lightning
and hear the loud rumble of thunder,

L.A.S.T. Revenge
IV.

Carl, on the other hand, was different. One would think that Carl was a homebody, and not an online dating debonair: A player, a man with two jobs, a nice car and nice apartment. I was thinking it was about time to play the player.

Tracking him down was kind of interesting. I found him at a hole in the wall where he spent four nights a week working as a bartender. It was called the Windjammer Restaurant & Lounge. When push came to shove, he even managed to be part-time DJ. He liked to date when he wasn't working, so I thought I would take advantage of one of his dates, or should I say 'dating him'.

I went to the public library and used one of their computers. I put together a nice dating profile and made sure that he would find that online. I described myself as somewhat attractive, but I didn't place a picture. I thought that would lend a little sense of mystery to a blind date. My profile name was Bobbie Kay and it stated that we'd have to meet somewhere in public.

He thought we should meet at a playground. I told him we would meet at 4:00 PM at the main mall downtown, and that we could get a bite to eat at the food court. I wrote that I would be standing inside near the revolving doors; look for a woman in a black dress. "I'll be the one holding the sign with your name on it."

Of course, I had no plans to be at that spot, I would be waiting in my dark blue Mustang in the back of the dimly lit parking garage to set up a quick walk-by hit. Now, being thoughtful, Carl stopped by a flower shop on his way to meet his blind date. So, when he pulled into the parking garage driving a fully loaded bright green Cadillac El Dorado convertible... well at least he didn't have the top down, and that's all that I needed.

Just as he was getting out, and had just barely opened the door with the flowers in his right hand I walked up from behind. I pulled out my .45 caliber, with silencer, and put a bullet in his left ear. Which knocked him back and laid him across the front seats. I was nice enough to close the door. The flowers were laying on the steering wheel and I left him like that. Lucky for me there were no people, only their parked cars.

43

The funny thing about Godfrey: as one of the members of the *beat-up Leslie club,* he made sure to humiliate me in some way – like pulling my pants down in front of everyone. One time he ran up and squirted my pants with a water gun to make look like I peed on myself. Well, while investigating him, I wound up flying to Hawaii and there, I found out that Godfrey had left home shortly after I did. He moved to Hawaii where he met and fell deeply infatuated with a woman who is half black and half Hawaiian. Her name is Mahina. She is a beautiful plus size model. They had a wonderful romantic affair, and afterwards she dumped him and went back to her husband, just as if she was taking a break from their marriage. This left Godfrey shocked and deeply depressed. As if that wasn't bad enough Godfrey, with my help and a note left in the right place, met Kai her six-foot-one, two-hundred-and-seventy-five pound husband, Kai found it necessary to punch Godfrey in the face, breaking his jaw.

After leaving the hospital Godfrey felt more deeply depressed, and did me a favor. He rented a hotel room ran a tub of nice warm water and got in it; he then slit both his wrists, and that's the way they found him.

I was on a flight flying first-class back to Buffalo.

I still remember how Johnny and Ronny were trying to see who could hit me the hardest. Lucky for me there was nothing to break in my stomach. It took a little doing, but I managed to get brothers Johnny and Ronnie by looking up their older brother Bill. He was working at the old corner store that back in the day the store was called Ethel's Confectionery

Now it's Marcy's grocery goodies – there's also a new laundromat down the block that also has Marcy's name on it. Bill and Marcy had became a couple. Twins Johnny and Ronnie still hung together, in front of the store. The twins had joined the Marines, but neither made it through Boot Camp, and they came right back to where they started. They still were wearing the freshly near-bald haircuts under worn baseball caps.

Marcy, not one to waste an opportunity, was quick to put Johnny and Ronnie to work as their delivery drivers. Bill had a white Ford F-360 pick-up truck that the boys used for deliveries. I thought this was a great chance to donate to charity and have the Twins deliver themselves up to me. There is a church that runs a homeless shelter and kitchen on the other side of town – First Shiloh Catholic Church. I made sure my five-hundred-dollar donation was of canned goods so both twins would work on that evening delivery. Marcy's was about to close for the day, and this was the last run of that shift. With so many cans they'd surely work it together so they could get done on time.

Even mother nature played her part with a little bit of lightning, a rumble of thunder and some rain. The boys drove over to the parking lot behind the kitchen where they could unload the truck. A nun was holding the door open for them raising an umbrella. While the fellas were unloading the truck. I was hiding and waiting, laying in a spot where I had a clear shot even from the dark wooded area behind the lit parking lot. I waited for them to unload. No one paid any attention to my rented dark blue Mustang parked in the back of the parking lot.

Nightmare Break-in

Ethel woke with a start, pulling the covers off in one sweeping move. She was sweating, heart racing, and breathing rapidly. This was not just a hot flash. Sitting up on the side of the bed, feet on the floor sliding into her slippers, the track star from her youth was ready to run – if one could run from a nightmare. It's not like she wouldn't try. There was still some of the spirited athlete left in her.

It's three AM, and she has to be up for work at six. His words and the sound of his voice, still echoing in her mind, "I don't want to hurt you but I will if I have too." The room was dark, she reached over to turn on the lamp and froze.

She heard the floorboards in the living room squeak. Not moving a muscle, her heart pounding again like it was about to jump out of her chest, fear gripped her every thought. Someone was here. She had an intruder, but was it him? She reached for her cell phone that wasn't there. Last night it had fallen to the floor when she plugged it in to recharge, and so she thought she'd just get it in the morning. She felt around trying to find a black phone in a dark room; it was somewhere under the bed, but where was it?

Other than some jewelry, a flat screen TV and some framed family pictures she didn't have anything of value. Her friends knew she lived alone and said she should be careful. They told her she should get a dog. She wasn't a dog person, but right now she wished for a couple of pit-bulls and a rottweiler.

The intruder made his way through the house and into her room before she could get under the bed and call 911. Surprised at her picking that moment to turn on the lamphe was startled. She screamed at him. "Get Out!! Leave!! I'm calling the cops!" She was screaming in hopes of waking her neighbors.

He didn't wear a mask. She saw his face, and to her surprise he looked like his father, and he had the same birthmark, too: a star just under his right earlobe that was about the size of a quarter. It looked like a tattoo or an earring just behind his jaw. He looked around for something worth taking. She looked at his face as he moved quickly around the room.

He said, "Look lady, I don't want to hurt you, but I will if I have too."

It was uncanny how the memories came flooding back. Saying nothing because she had screamed herself hoarse, and not moving other than to cover herself a little better with the blanket, she stood there. She had seen his birthmark. He had his father's eyes and hair and knew she had seen it only once before. He was quick and left the way he had come in. He didn't trash the place or harm her in any way.

She called the police and gave them a description of the man who somehow looked very familiar. The very next day she changed the locks and had a new deadbolt put in the front door. She joined the neighborhood watch program for her own peace of mind.

It was four months and the night of a full moon when she had another nightmare. She woke up sweating, and her heart pounding in her chest. This time he said in her dream, "I'll bet you thought you'd never see me again." Only, he was already standing in her bedroom, standing right in front of the bed, startling her as she sat up. She practically jumped out of her skin, placing a hand on her chest. This time she managed not to scream. Looking right in his eyes as he stood there saying, "I'll bet you thought you'd never see me again. I heard it said that we tend to return to the scene of a crime. So look, I'll just take the money and go." He took the crumpled up 25 dollars cash that she was foolish enough to leave out on her dresser right next to her cell phone.

She looked at his birthmark again as he made his way out, dropping the cell phone battery at the door of her house. Just the thought that he was already in the house and could have done anything to her left her with more than a few sleepless nights. She found help in the form of a bottle of Gray Goose vodka. She'd get herself a drink and try to relax. However when she did sleep she was busy dreaming of him. This would stay with her for some time.

Just as she was getting over her fear of this man breaking into her life she remembered where she first saw that birthmark. She was sixty-five years old now, and the memories of her first kiss soon after her first crush came back like an old friend
returning for a visit.

It was her summer of love. His name was Henry but everybody called him Hank. He'd been away at a private school and came home for summer vacation when he would work for his uncle who was a photographer. He fell in love at first sight. He was turning eighteen and Ethel, a former tomboy, had just turned seventeen, but already had the full figure of a voluptuous woman. This is the day she was tired of wearing floppy, over-sized t-shirts and baseball caps. She wanted to wear something to show off her shape.

Looking in the mirror, she thought this outfit was cute. A nice light blue blouse, some hip hugging jeans and sandals. Ethel painted her nails to match her blouse. Taking the hairpins out and combing her almost jet-black hair, she let it fall down to the middle of her back. She thought she looked ok, but she was drop dead gorgeous; she just didn't know it. Henry really was the boy next door. When he saw the vision that stepped out of her front door and walk to the mailbox to get the mail – somehow "WOW!" just didn't seem to cover it. Henry's uncle, seeing this, said he should go get the mail as he pushed him, "and here, take a camera with you see if you can take some pictures of her." Hank's uncle knew there was no film in the camera. The rest was a matter of romantic history: boy meets girl.

It would be six months before Ethel had her next nightmare. She woke up sweating with her
heart pounding in her chest, breathing rapidly. In her dream she heard him say, "You know this is becoming a habit." She had to agree.

Well, at least he wasn't waiting for her when she woke up this time. She waited for him to come in. He came in the house as if he had a key. He seemed to be a recreational thief; he was in her bathroom looking through her medicine cabinet. He didn't find anything of street value, nor any quick money. Other than estrogen tablets and medication for hypertension she was a healthy woman.

He came in her bedroom like a bully looking to beat up somebody. He looked frustrated as he said, "You know this is becoming a habit?"

Ethel asked him, "Why do you keep coming here anyway? Is this how you get your kicks? Or are you hooked on drugs or something?" She looked at him and said, "You may not believe me, but you and I share a history. I think you may want to sit down for this; I am not going to call the cops I promise." He thought she was crazy, and that maybe he'd humor her while he looked around for something to take.

She motioned for him to sit on the bed. She looked at him and spoke, "I know that birthmark." Looking in her eyes as he touched his neck with his right hand. "You may not believe me, but I'm your Mother... You were brought into this world as the result of young love. One day I'd like to tell you about your father, or what I knew of him. Back then the world wasn't like it is now. Our parents were old fashioned, they kept me hidden from the neighbors, and when it was time your father was sent back to boarding school, and I never heard from him again. My parents took me to the hospital. I only saw you for a moment;
they wouldn't let me hold you. You were born with that birthmark."

Looking at this woman, not sure what he wanted to say or do, he got up and left. A year went by and on Mother's Day. A box of chocolates, some red roses with a card and small box was delivered. The card had an apology and a request with a phone number. The box held everything that was taken.

I Came to Play

Back in the day, before cell phones, before B.D.U.s, the Army's new Battle Dress Uniform, I would say somewhere around 1982; It, for me, was a very good year.

I was in the army, being all that I could be: a warrior by day, a former Artillery man turned records clerk, a modern-day Clark Kent, a brother and a gentlemen of color. I was dealing with my own version of the show The Office as Specialist Robert Lee Kinard, but four nights a week, I was Dee Jay Bobby K, "The one to know!" Playing the music that makes the difference!

For me this was a dream come true – A fantasy fulfilled – and for fifteen years, I was living that dream. After playing and mixing music for the other Dee Jay's as a volunteer a manager saw that I was the real talent and hired me to work part-time. I was working at the Fort Eustis N.C.O. (Non-Commissioned Officer) club in Virginia. A brand-new building with three rooms built for sound, it had a lounge on each end and a main ballroom in the middle. As a disc jockey I was all about a party and ready to throw down. There's something about having brand new stereo equipment that makes me feel like a kid with a brand-new toy. The DJ's console consisted of two SL 1200 mk2 Technics turn tables, one on each side; they were the best on the market. There was a mixer in the middle and the lighting controls right above the mixer. What's a ballroom without a mirrored ball and other lighting effects directly over the dance floor? There were four very large Bose speakers over the dance floor, and sixteen two-foot Sansui speakers just below the ceiling around the tops of the walls of the ballroom. One could hear and feel the music.

That night I was on stage
behind the turn tables mixing music without a care
when a fine woman walks up.

She wants to hear her song;
      makes me glad I was standing there.
      She finds a reason to tell me
      that she's not wearing underwear.
I watch her do a little dance and
      shake what mother nature made.
I was half way thinking I might even get laid.
She wore sensible shoes and a tight red mini.
Her legs were nice, but I thought she was too skinny.

There was a feeling in the air,
      a feeling in the room's atmosphere.
The excitement like an electric charge that said,
      "Let's go do it,
      let's get to it"
As the night went on, I had the spot lights moving
      the Bass was booming.
The crowd was jumping and the place was packed.

Naughty by Nature's "Hip Hop Hooray",
then L. L. Cool Jay's "I'm Bad",
I'd spin Eric Bee's "Paid in Full",
and Public Enemy's "Bring the Noise".
Cut in some fast moving house music.
Mix in some alternative with plenty of sound effects.
I open the Mic to speak to the crowd to say,
      "I'm Dee Jay Bobby K and I came to play!
"Alright fellas where my dogs at?
      Where my dogs at?"
All the men in the room would start barking.
Let's see if we can get through tonight
      without someone starting a fight.

"Can I get a soul clap!" I said, "Now, the ladies!
        Who wanted these songs?!"
        Don't have any panties on!"

Laughter can be heard, as they clap to the beat.
        I see a few faces smile and blush,
        trying to hide by looking towards the feet.
"Ladies, if there's no shame
                in your game
        let me hear you scream!"
All the women would scream,
some would scream like their lives were in danger.

Then I'd play some hot Reggae music
        Shaba Ranks and Maxi Priest.
More people moving to the floor
        it's now a moving crush.
For a few minutes, everyone wants to be a Jamaican.
People danced where they were,
        between the tables or standing along the walls.
Everybody, and I mean everybody, is having a ball.
The fighting drunks are out in the foyer,
                Security makes a 911 call.
The Fire Marshal was already there,
                in managers ear.
Telling him, "You have too many people in the building.
        This is a fire hazard.
You must get some of these people out of here!"
"Fine! Says the manager.
        We can start with all these drunks right here!"

(Mean while back in the Ballroom)
I said, "Alright people! It's after one

lets have some fun!
If you're from anywhere but here
    wave your hands in the air!
    wave them like you just don't care!
Let me hear the east coast make some noise!"
    and they'd yell at me for a few seconds.
Then I'd say,
    "Is it true the Mid-west
        is the best?"
And they too yelled.
Then I just say, "West Coast in the house!"
    and we had them yelling too.

Then I'd start a Chant and the crowd would run with it.
"The roof! The roof! The roof is on fire!!" and the crowd on the
dance floor would say,
    "We don't need no water, let the Mothafucka burn! Burn,
Mothafucka, burn!" They'd repeat this, two or three times while
I'm playing a song called Planet Rock followed by Play at Your Risk.
Then, I take them back in time with
Parliament's Flash Light.

This would go on for a little while,
    you'd think this would go out of style.
It was like a sauna in the ballroom,
    but nobody wanted to leave
The manager opened the door between
    the ballroom and lounge – let some air
    and people move between rooms.
That was my cue to slow down the music
    with some Luther Vandross,
    and Boys II Men.
There was a lot of people who wanted to get close

some who needed to get a room.

If you weren't one of the couples on the dance floor while the
music was slow was best time to get to the bar. I'd open the
Microphone with a joke; saying, "Somebody smells horny!" This
had some couples laughing, and I'd add, "you know who you are,"
and the crowd would laugh even more. Most of the night, I had a
line of people making requests, I was taking them all and doing my
best. I couldn't go one night without playing "The Electric Slide".
The song had everybody moving, tables had to pushed back. We
also had those slide experts who could move opposite of the crowd
without missing a beat. It was a smooth mesh of people.

I had the Dee Jay wannabes
      begging for a chance to play,
but for some of them it was not a good day.
The same said for the rap star wannabes,
      begging for a chance to get on the Mic
(Some of them had to much grit.)
One lovely lady asks for her song
      and then struck her tongue in my ear.
      She was really fine,
      and drunk out of her mind,
      but a friend gave me a warning.
I put my hands back on the turn tables,
      moving the crowd
      until about 2:30 or 300 in the morning

Because I came to play.

L.A.S.T. Revenge
finalé.

I was set up with my rifle and silencer. The rain was coming down hard. I waited until the Nun had closed the back door. With the front of the truck facing me and Johnny sitting behind steering wheel I put a bullet in the front right tire. He got out to see about the flat tire, just as he knelt down to look at the now flat tire. He didn't see it coming, I put a bullet in his head. Johnny slumped over and leaned on the truck.

At that time Ronny was walking up to get into the right side of the truck, so he did not see Johnny go down. After a couple of minutes, he got out and walked around the truck to see what was up with Johnny. He cried out, "Johnny!" and went down on one knee to see about his brother, and I put a bullet in the back of his head. He, too, slumped over, leaning on his brother. I left them there in the rain.

It kept raining. Now that I had gotten all of my former teenage bullies I thought the only nice thing to do was to turn myself in. So, I got in my car and drove to the county sheriff's office, where I was stopped at the door. I was dressed in Army olive drab and camouflage clothing, you see, and a sheriff's deputy stopped me at the door and said, "Can I help you?"

I said, "Yes, you sure can. I'd like to turn myself in."

He said, "Let me frisk you, and then you can come in and talk about it."

"Well, sir," I replied, "you should know that all my weapons are in my car, the dark blue Mustang over there."

So, the deputy let me walk in and I'm sure I gave them an ear full with my confession. I told them again that the weapons I used were in the car in their parking lot and, along with the keys to the car, I gave them a brief history: my past and why I felt it necessary to take my revenge this late. It didn't take them long to match me up with what I had described as revenge on my part.

The sheriff said I, "Would've made one hell of an investigator," had I not killed those men. He added that if I had killed the guy in Hawaii this would be under the FBI's jurisdiction. I told them it just shows that, with life, what goes around eventually comes around.

Now with our justice system being the way it is, it took them all of five months to get me into court and on to sentencing. The families of the men I killed were there also, I'll bet that they were not happy that New York State no longer had the death penalty. The judge said that since I had turned myself in peacefully, it was the decision of the court that I, Leslie Alan Samuel-Tailer would hereby be sentenced to twnety-five years to life – and may God have mercy on my soul. He struck the gavel twice, "Court is adjourned."

I was escorted out in handcuffs to serve my time in prison. If looks could kill, I would have been executed by all of the family members before I was walked out the court room.

Jonathan said, "Wait, you said you had enough money to do what you did. Now that you've served your twenty-five years is there anything left?"

"Well, while I was incarcerated I stayed in contact with my financial institutions, and I still have a nest egg to play with. The sheriff said that had I not killed those men I would've made one hell of an investigator. Now that I'm almost 50 years old and in my retirement I will need something to do. So, I think I'll look into becoming a private investigator."

I can just see it
L.A.S.T. Investigations

colophon
Brought to you by Wider Perspectives Publishing, care of James Wilson, with the mission of advancing the poetry and creative community of Hampton Roads, Virginia.

See our production of works from ...

Chichi Iwuorie
Symay Rhodes
Tanya Cunningham-Jones
          (Scientific Eve)
Terra Leigh
Ray Simmons
Samantha Borders-Shoemaker
J. Scott Wilson (TEECH!)
Charles Wilson
Gloria Darlene Mann
Neil Spirtas
Jorge Mendez & JT Williams
Sarah Eileen Williams
Stephanie Diana (Noftz)
the Hampton Roads
          Artistic Collective
Jason Brown (Drk Mtr)
Martina Champion

Tony Broadway
Zach Crowe
Ken Sutton
Crickyt J. Expression
Lisa M. Kendrick
Cassandra IsFree
Nich (Nicholis Williams)
Samantha Geovjian Clarke
Natalie Morison-Uzzle
Gus Woodward II
Patsy Bickerstaff

Catherine TL Hodges

Jack Cassada

Dezz

... and others to come soon.

We promote and support the artists of the 757
from the seats, from the stands,
from the snapping fingers andclapping hands
from the pages, and the stages
and now we pass them forth
to the ages

Check for the above artists on
FaceBook, the Virginia Poetry
Online channel on YouTube,
and other social media.